G6 W BATTLE OF PAINTBALL HILL

Written by Colin M. Moore

ISBN 978-1-7377456-3-1

Illustrated by Colin M. Moore.
Digitized by Aria Jones.

LCCN 2022916711

10 9 8 7 6 4 5 3 2 1

Sounds of paintballs splattered against the roof of our team's bunker. Splash! Splash! Splash! Paint-filled water balloons exploded, all around us. *My name's Levi, one of the many kids participating in this crazy paintball war.* "What do we do?" My best friend Lexi asked. "We're all out of paint balloons to launch, and most of our paint guns are out too!" *Oh-no, that's bad! What to do?*

All the excitement made me tired. After a few yawns, I began to drift off to sleep and daydream about how this whole crazy paintball war began and how silly the reason was...

1

We were outside on the neighborhood playground, and Lexi and I were just chilling out, playing a nice quiet game of chess.

Suddenly I heard, "Hey losers!" Tyler, the school bully, walked toward us with his gang of rebels behind him. "You two are going to pay for making me drench myself in water at school!"

He was referring to last week at school, when me and Lexi were going to get a drink of water from the water fountain at the same time he was drinking. I bumped into him by accident, causing him to drench himself. Then Lexi came out of the girls locker room and bumped him again, causing him to soak himself even more.

"Dude, we are sorry about that. We'll make it up to you," I said, trying to stay out of a fight. "It's not about the water fountain situation," he said. "It's about showing you who's boss! I challenge you to a paintball war!" Lexi was about to say no, but I'm not the type of guy that shies away from a challenge. "Challenge accepted!" I said.

2

"What are you doing?" Lexi whispered. I gave her a wink and muttered, "I've always wanted to play paintball." Lexi gave me a disapproving look and we both snapped our attention back to Tyler. "You have one day to gather your team and build your fort," Tyler said. "Good luck...NOT!"

As soon as Tyler left, we started to gather up all our friends for our team and started to make our fort. We grabbed some old camping tents, a bunch of cardboard boxes, some raggedy old towels, and a tree branch barrier to create a heavily fortified tent bunker with a cardboard box wall surrounding it. We named our team, THE G6 WARRIORS (G6 for grade six).

"It's a beauty, isn't it?" I asked Lexi. She nodded and stared in awe of our creation. One of our warriors, Ryan, had the brilliant idea to make paint-filled balloon catapults. We loaded the catapults with paint balloons and headed home for the night.

The next morning, we were shocked and slightly scared to find a huge fort, created by the opposing team (Team Shadow; the black team).

"Hey losers! Today, you're actually going to be losers!" Tyler taunted, his team behind him. "Here are the rules," I said, noticing Tyler looking bored as I spoke. "If you get hit by paint, you're out! Simple! Now, everybody, get into your forts!" Lexi, me, and the rest of my team rushed into our fort to get our armor on, ready the slingshot, and load the paint guns.

A few moments later, I heard a loud whistling sound coming from across the field we were playing on. "Do you hear that?" Lexi asked. I nodded and poked my head outside the bunker. "Everybody get down!" I said. Instantly, paint balloons exploded on our base, splattering everything. SPLAT! SLPAT! SPLAT!

"They must have copied our catapults!" I said. "You cheaters!" Lexi shouted. "Lexi, I need you and the rest of the team to operate the catapults!" I said. "Okay!" she said, trying to talk over the sound of blasting paint balloons and paint guns shooting through the air. "You, you, and you come with me," I said, pointing to three warriors.

We suited up in our armor and paint guns, and charged outside, shooting anyone in a black shirt. "Gah!" A kid in my squad yelled. His name was Rico and I just figured out why he yelled. He was hit!

"Oh-no!" he said. "Go on without me, my friends! I shall go home to my father in the sky." He runs away, in dramatic Rico fashion (Rico is in the school drama club).

We shot down a lot of the other teams' members, but we were easily outnumbered. There were about fifteen of us and twenty-two of them. I only wanted to bring a few kids into battle with me, so that way I could limit the loss of our warriors.

Another wave of paint balloons flew toward us. Luckily, we also carried trashcan lid shields on our backs. "Shields up!" I yelled.

G6 **Warriors**(Main Players)

1 Levi	2 Lexi	3 Ryan	4 Jay	5 Rachel	6 Lila
7 Rico	8 Logan	9 Rose	10 Tasha	11 Clinton	12 Zack

The three of us pulled out our shields and hunched together to take cover, just before the balloons splattered us. SPLAASSSH!! The balloons exploded around us like bombs.

A few Team Shadow members saw us trying to avoid the attack and started to fire. I was able to shield myself from the attack. "Fall back! I repeat, fall back! Tactical retreat is in order!" We all ran back to the fort, but in the process, a kid named Lila was shot, black and blue paint oozed down her face.

"Ouch, that hurt! Well, I guess I'm out then," Lila said. "I'm going home to wash the paint out of my hair. Win this war for me, will you?" I gave her a nod and a smile, and the rest of us ambled towards our bunker. Lexi was waiting for me outside of the fort.

"While you were gone, I got Zack and Logan to capture this guy from Team Shadow," Lexi said. "Take one of Team Shadow's warriors prisoner?" I asked, my eyebrows raised in contemplation. "Nice thinking Lexi! Bring him in boys."

Zack and Logan brought out a kid from the back of the bunker. His hands were tied together, so I wasn't worried about him trying any funny business. "Spill the beans, we know you and your team snuck into our fort and copied our catapults! Tell us now!" I yelled.

"I'm not telling you anything!" The guy said. I grabbed a paint gun and put it right to his chest. "Talk now or else!" I said, trying to be as terrifying as possible. *Guess what? My act didn't work.*

"Like I'm going to tell that information to a coward like you," he sneered. "You're the coward here, not me," I said. "You're too scared to tell us because you think you'll get in trouble!" That seemed to hit his core. He paused, looked around the bunker, and eventually agreed to tell us.

"Tyler sent me on a mission to gather information on your fort," the guy said. This all happened last night, so we wouldn't get caught," he went on to explain. "After studying your short-range catapults, we built more powerful, long-range slingshots. You know everything now. Let me go," he said, struggling to get out of the rope.

"What is your name?" I asked. "My name is Nolan," he grumbled.

"Okay Nolan, I'm going to give you a one-time offer. You could go back to your team and probably get shot in battle fighting for Tyler's Team Shadow, or you can join The G6 Warriors and win. Take your pick," I said, putting out my hand.
He shook my hand and said, "Deal!"

"Uh-oh!" Lexi said, "We're out of paint balloons to launch!"
Oh-no, that's bad! What to do? I looked outside the bunker and besides the paint chaos, I saw a distant hill to the left of our base. "If we can get to that hill over there, we may just have a slight advantage!"

"How about a few of us go check it out?" Lexi suggested, eyeballing the hill. From the bottom it looked more like a mountain. "Great idea," I replied. "Move out as soon as possible." I watched as Lexi and our squad geared up and moved out.

Ten minutes later....

One of the G6 Warriors, named Rose, nosedived into our bunker, looking defeated. "What happened? Where's the rest of the squad?" I asked. "We were ambushed! Everyone else was caught and taken prisoner for interrogation!" Rose said in dismay.

"I'm going after them," I said audaciously. "Does anybody have some camouflage armor I can have?"

"I do, and I'm going with you," Nolan said, holding up the camo armor. "I know Team Shadow's fort better than anybody. I even know it better than Tyler because I'm the one who came up with the blueprints. Plus, I want to prove my loyalty to the team." I nodded, and we both put on our armor.

"Grab the smaller paint guns," I said. "Why?" Nolan asked. "They're low power and don't have that far of a firing range," I answered.

On a quest to find Team Shadow's fort, Nolan and I walked through the trees, slipping in and out of the shadows.

We walked for a while before we spotted their black, blanket covered fort. Armed and ready for battle, there were two Team Shadow members standing guard.

"Alright Nolan, what's the best way to get into this fortress?" I asked. "There's an emergency exit in the back of the fort. We penetrate it that way," Nolan said.

Like cunning cats, we crept to the back of Team Shadow's fort, and entered through the back door, just like Nolan said. Surprisingly, their bunker was made of actual wood! We started to listen through the doors. With a few fails, and two close calls of being seen, we heard Tyler questioning our teammates from behind a red door.

We slowly opened the door and slipped inside unnoticed. The door led to a staircase, which led to an opening on the roof of their fort. I saw what Tyler was doing. All tied to different poles, were members of our team! They were tied up about eighteen feet from Nolan and me.

"Tell us what your team is up to or else!" Tyler said. "Yeah right! We'll never say a word," Lexi said, fighting to get loose. "I know you took one of my warriors prisoner. Tell me, did he give away any information on my team?" Tyler asked.

Nolan stepped out of the shadows. "Not only did I tell them everything, but I'm now on the winning team!" Nolan said. "I'm a G6 WARRIOR!"

"You traitor!" Tyler yelled indignantly. "You're the traitor, not me," Nolan said. "Last night, when we were building this very fort, did you help? NO! We were out there risking our lives. What did you do? You sat down in that little hammock of yours rocking back and forth, back and forth, then you fell asleep! You don't treat us like we're a part of your team, you treat us like peasants! I'm done with you!"

That kid is braver than I'll ever be, I thought. Standing up to that bully the way he did took real guts!

"Nice speech kid, but you're no match for me. Get him!" Tyler commanded to his squad. "Come and get me!" Nolan said.

Nolan rushed down to the door we entered through with a Team Shadow member right on his trail. The commotion and the camo suit helped me stay out of sight. I jumped out of hiding and rushed over to my friends.

"Levi?" Lexi said, like she could not believe her eyes. "I thought you would never come for us!" I untied her hands first. "Untie everybody else. I need to go and help Nolan," I said. "We're coming too," Lexi said.

"No," I protested. "If I get hit, then you're our only hope of winning this war."

"We'll cover you as you guys' escape," a warrior named Jake said." The others nodded in agreement.

I looked around and saw a box. It was filled with paint balloon satchels. "You guys can use these!" I said, handing them a satchel and grabbing one of my own.

We ran down to the entrance and found, six or seven Team Shadow warriors going against Nolan. I had to hand it to the kid, he was doing surprisingly good dodging Team Shadow's shots, but I knew it was only a matter of time before he got splattered with paint.

"Hey you guys!" G6 Warrior member Tasha shouted, alarming the other team. Almost every Team Shadow warrior turned around and as soon as they did, Clinton, Logan, and Tasha threw their balloons, splatting almost every Team Shadow member.

"Go!" Clinton yelled. We ran over to Nolan who was still dodging two of Team Shadow's warriors who didn't turn their heads. Lexi threw the only two paint balloons she had left, splashing it all over the rival team. Lexi, Nolan, and I ran to the emergency exit.

Once we reached the door, I slammed it shut and held it there so the Team Shadow members couldn't get to us. "Open this door," Dereck, from Team Shadow yelled.

"You can't hold the door closed forever dude!" Lexi said. "I can hold it long enough for you two to get back to the rest of the team!" I said. "What? No! We're not leaving you!" Lexi said. "We're out of options! You have to get back and lead the..."

"I'll hold them off," Nolan interrupted. "I was on the wrong side for too long. It's time I do some good for the team."

I nodded and then we shook hands. "It's been an honor to fight by your side," I said. Nolan smiled and turned. Lexi and I escaped into the woods.

 I stood at the edge of the forest, watching Nolan. Once Nolan let go of the door, all the Team Shadow warriors fell through, leaving them helpless as Nolan shot them down. I watched him bravely fight off every black warrior, but soon, the paint balloon launchers on Team Shadow spotted him and started shooting at him. He tried to run, but there was too much chaos around. He lost his balance, dropped his shield, and stumbled to the ground. Once his former team members noticed that Nolan was unarmed and completely helpless, they shot him down like mad.

I couldn't bear what I was seeing. Luckily, Lexi pulled me away. "Come on Levi! It's too late for Nolan now," she said. I nodded, but that didn't change what I felt in that moment.

We stopped when we got to the middle of the battlefield. There was no more fighting! And our team? They did what they were told like good warriors, and they conquered the hill!

We ran up the slope and gave high fives to everybody, but the celebration didn't last long. After about a minute, every Team Shadow warrior came out of their fort, including Tyler, who was in the center of the army.

"Attack!" Tyler shouted. "Shields up!" I yelled. Five members of our team lifted their shields to create a shield wall, while the other fifteen warriors broke out their paint guns and started shooting like there was no tomorrow.

Because we had the high ground, we were able to hit more kids. Team Shadow, on the other hand, had to climb and shoot at the same time, so their attacks weren't accurate, and they were being shot down; one by one.

For a short moment, I felt victorious, but that feeling quickly dissipated.

Little by little, G6 Warriors from the back of the line started to get shot, which is weird because, well, they were in the back! I looked off to the side and figured out what was happening. "Guys! They're not just in front of us, they're behind us too!" I shouted.

There were four Team Shadow warriors on the other side of the hill and somehow, two of those warriors were in paintball launching tanks! Did you hear me? They were in military style tanks!

In a panic, I dumped my paint balloons on them. Probably not the best option, but the only idea I had. I hit two of those warriors, but (as you probably guessed) they weren't the tank operators. One tank fired and grazed the top of my battle mask, knocking it off, and leaving me completely exposed.

"Don't worry, help is on the way!" I heard two voices say in unison. Jumping in front of me were the twins, Jay and Rachel. They dodged the attacks and then they each jumped up on a tank, practically in sync, opened the hatches, and then took out the drivers inside.

With that problem out of the way, I turned around and the G6 Warriors had lost about a quarter of their members. Team Shadow had lost about half!

Lexi and I were the only ones left on our team, and Tyler was the only one on his. Tyler quickly took out his paint gun and shot directly at me, but just as I prepared for the worst, Lexi pushed me to the side and sacrificed herself for me.

"Nooooooo!" I screamed. "Go!" Lexi said, heading back to our base, "Finish this war!"

Now, without Lexi, it felt like a cowboy showdown from a wild wild west movie. I tried to shoot, but nothing happened.

"Oh-no! I'm out of ammo!" I shouted. Tyler shot at me while laughing a villainous laugh. I pulled out my shield just in time to block the attack.

"You can't hide behind that shield forever!" Tyler yelled. "You'll have to make your move sooner or later!" I knew he was right, even though I really wished he wasn't.

I placed my free hand into my pocket, feeling defeated. Squish. Squish. Squish. I felt something. I pulled out my hand and...WHOA! The very last paint balloon! This was my last hope. I raised the balloon up to my chin and shot it over my head. Tyler never saw it coming. SPLAT! Tyler got soaked in paint before he realized what I had done. "We won! We won!" I screamed.

Lexi came and gave me the biggest hug of my life. Then the rest of the G6 Warriors came and lifted me into the air, carrying me down the hill where Nolan was waiting.

"Those were some pretty cool moves back there," he said. "You're not too bad yourself," I said. We bumped fists; the way new friends do.

"What should we do to celebrate our victory?" Lila asked. There was a moment of silence until... "My dad owns an arcade; we can go there!" Nolan said.

19

Lexi, Nolan and I sat at a table in the arcade eating pizza. "Do you guys think Tyler is mad at us for winning?" I asked. "That kid will stop at nothing to get what he wants," Nolan said. "In this case, he wants revenge."

That answer really gave me a chill down my spine. Lexi could tell I looked worried. "But don't worry Levi! Whatever happens, I got your back," Lexi said. "Same here," Nolan echoed.

"Thanks guys," I said with a smile. Nolan is right, Tyler will come for his revenge, but as long as the G6 Warriors are by my side, I feel like I can do anything.

Made in the USA
Coppell, TX
26 January 2023

11742798R10016